Extra Lessons

Londa Cele

Published by Londa Cele, 2023.

EXTRA LESSONS

First edition. March 24, 2023.

Copyright © 2023 Londa Cele.

ISBN: 979-8223607618

Written by Londa Cele.

1

When people hear the word abuse, the first image that comes to mind is of a woman splayed on the floor like spilt milk. The silhouette of a drunk man with his belt soaring above his head and a smirk bearing across his face before bringing it down and a toddler crunched up in the corner with their hands around their face but Sipho was none of those things. Matter of fact, he was an ordinary boy with the only extraordinary thing about him being the fact that he had finished high school a year earlier than his peers. Light-skinned and kept to himself. Sure, he had problems, anybody shaped like a lollipop would, but he accepted how the world would deem fit to disrespect him because of the way he looked. That, and he lived with his Aunt Rebecca, a police officer in need of a therapist but didn't want to admit it. Whether it was a race thing or related to her job, she was always in a foul mood with the only reason she agreed to share her home with her nephew in the first place being how much she valued education.

"Sipho," his Aunt shouted.

Sipho hurried downstairs. Being summoned more than once was forbidden. He jumped off his bed, ignoring the fact that he'd hurt his knee, and hurried toward the sound of her voice to find her watching a medical series in the lounge. "Yes, Aunty?"

She looked up at him and he at her, but because of the way he was raised, staring back at her was deemed disrespectful.

"Look at me," she said and his shoulders slumped with defeat. There was not much that he could do, even if he could outrun her toward her service pistol.

"Sipho. I said look at me. I won't tell you again,"

"Yes Aunty," looking up at her, his eyes squeezed with emotion as they opened, glaring up at her.

"There we go. Now was that so hard, Mmm?"

"No," Sipho growled.

"Ooh, so manly," she said, resting a manicured finger on the tip of her fat lips. "I love the fire in your eyes, it's got me feeling hot. In fact, go get me a glass of water,"

Sipho sighed, he knew exactly what that meant. This wasn't the first time this would happen nor would it be the last, all he could do was let her finish, write about how it made him feel and try not to let it get to him. Despite being her bitch, he wouldn't allow her to make him cry like she had done the previous night. She'd taken things way too far. Any other male in his shoes would call him insane for passing up such a chance but they weren't in his shoes, so all they had to do was shut up.

"Sipho?"

Shock and fear comforted each other in his head. "coming," he said, appearing around a corner with a glass of water. In his absence, a blue pill and his Aunt's service pistol were waiting patiently for the glass to join them.

"You know what to do, I can't spoon-feed you everything. You already live in my house rent-free, what more do you want?"

Sipho knew that his Aunt became like this when her loins couldn't agree on something. At first, her words were hurtful, his feelings cast aside, and she didn't even care what effect they'd have on a growing teenager but as time went on, they became as mundane as taking out the trash on Thursday. With the pill in one hand and the glass of water in the other, Sipho united the two in his mouth before showing her the evidence of their union with a wide open mouth for her to inspect. With her satisfied, he disappeared, out of sight and out of mind. He'd have an hour, give or take before he'd have to visit her again and join her as she played with her toys. It meant he had just enough time to get started on his assignment. It was sad, almost torturous and before he knew it, the sound of his stopwatch filled his room to remind him that it was time. When he headed to his Aunt's bedroom, his Aunt was in nothing but a nightgown and lingerie. She slid off the bed and nursed Sipho to the edge of her bed where his shorts and underwear found their way to the ground. As his Aunt's nails danced over his naked body, Sipho's eyes fluttered shut. To her and her ego, it meant that it was time to pull out the toys. Whereas for Sipho, it was time to pick a door and pick a way to kill himself, his Aunt's gun seemed like a huge temptation. He knew where it stayed and everything, all he needed was the courage to steal it. He tried his level best to ignore her nails as they danced between the inside of his thighs, but he couldn't stop himself from twitching as he felt them tickle him. The silence that ensued soon after, the cold that came with the application of lube for his Aunt's favourite toy, the penis pump. As she tortured him, forcing blood from the rest of his body to go to the tip of his penis even though it didn't want to, each pump caused the blood from his brain to vanish. She soon tossed the toy and wrapped her hand around his erect penis, forcing him to look at her as she stroked it up and down.

Sipho was forced to watch as his Aunt sucked him off, her mouth getting wetter the more he moaned in discomfort and squirmed uncomfortably. All the while she practised her dick-sucking skills on a child who couldn't protest because of how many times they'd been threatened to be shot if he spoke out. She didn't care, as long as she enjoyed herself. In reality, she'd never physically harm him and if things did turn sour, all she had to do was deny it... not that he'd be able to prove it. That said, she'd miss his large appendage, which is why she was on her knees, praising it, practising the art of being gag-reflex-free. That, and she was doing him a favour by teaching him how to use it. Besides, he'd come back later in life and thank her. She knew this because of how his eyes would roll back when she'd look up at him. She'd then removed him from her mouth and gently spread him across her bed. Sipho wasn't rough, he wasn't a spanker nor a choker, but they'd get there; they had time, four years if he failed nothing during his tenure at university.

Sipho hated what was about to come next but he didn't have a choice, as long as he lived under her roof, he'd live in fear, wishing that he had the courage to place that gun to the side of his head and pull the trigger, let his mind spill out his head like the contents she liked to suck of out his head. His Aunt would toy, tease, and torture the cumshots out of him. He would last hours in this state and she would take full advantage of those hours, forcing him into toe-curling experiences but never allowing him to release. First with foreplay, if it wasn't with her toys, be it the penis pumps or penis rings she'd force him to wear, then with all the jobs, be it hand or blown that would compete with one another. His voice used to give away his imminent finish, so she'd stop. Now, she'd count on his body to twitch no matter how hard he tried to stay still, rendering his efforts pointless.

2

"Sipho, can you stay behind?" Miss De Wet asked as the class shuffled between elongated desks towards the door and the freedom that lay beyond her lecture. Sipho growled but did what he was told, his upbringing served as his kryptonite. It was times like these he wished he was still in matric like the rest of his friends that he hadn't finished high school because people like De Wet wouldn't single him out. "Yes, Ma'am?" He asked when arriving at the bottom.

"I won't keep you long, I'm sure you've got places to be. Look, you're a bright student, but I don't see it here in my class and that's not what I called you down here for. I'm more concerned with-"

"No," Sipho thought, she mustn't say it. 'la-la-la' he sang, slowly moving his body towards the door while his body kept her attention with mmm's and yes ma'am's.

"I rarely do this," she said, blocking his way out. "But I can see whatever you are going through is affecting you based on how you've failed my assignment, which is something you'd never do. I've known you for three-quarters of a year now and I can make that assumption with confidence now. I know the concept of a university may be new to you and I don't know what you may have heard outside these walls but I need you to know that you can talk to us as lectures. We are people."

"Thank you, ma'am, I'll keep that in mind," Sipho nodded before trying to push his way past his teacher.

"Sipho, listen." Miss De Wet's voice went down an octave and Sipho shuddered. "I can't speak for other teachers but as a qualified psychologist I can say with confidence whatever you're harbouring inside, forget about it eating you up inside, it poses a serious risk to your health. A serious one as well, think along the lines of a heart attack." She lied, taking a step towards him in an effort to comfort him but he immediately took two steps back.

Sipho never expected this. Surprise took him. More so, because it was coming from an adult. He didn't know what to do, he'd lived his life avoiding extended periods of interaction with people to avoid finding himself in this very position and yet here he was, in the very position he worked so hard to avoid. The next best thing was to keep it together. All his problems weighed heavily on his chest like someone trying their best not to vomit despite it teasing to come out leaving an after-taste at the back of their throat which on its own triggered the gag reflex.

Sipho slammed his head against the blackboard, and covered his face with his hands, dragging chalk down with him as he slid down it as though they had shot him. "I can't ma'am."

"Are you okay?"

Those were the words that broke the camel's back, as the saying goes. Sipho shook his head in silence. His eyes burned and he fought back tears, each sniff of his nose failing even with the help of gravity. When he faced his teacher, they ab-sailed down toward his nose. A part of him told him to wipe his face and look decent, not to look weak in front of a woman, but he was too far gone. The fact that she could see something was wrong with him and took the time out to single him out and corner him much like his Aunt until he spoke was a sign that he needed help. That he needed to talk to someone. The question was, was he going to accept it? Or was Miss De Wet one of her Aunt's spies placed to check if he'd keep his mouth shut? He promised he wouldn't and if she'd ever found out that he did... all that filled his mind was that gun that lay next to that glass of water. Sipho shook his head, dislodging more tears in the process. "I'm sorry I can't," he wheezed.

***

When Sipho arrived home, there was pizza in the fridge and a note from his Aunt letting him know that she'd be working late. Any other 18-year-old male his age would kick his shoes to one side, put the radio on to the max and pull out the Vaseline or lube of choice to use alongside their favourite porn. But Sipho couldn't do that, not while he still lived with his Aunt, not while she was still a cop and most importantly, not while she was still alive. The thought of her made him shudder, and he lost his appetite, annoyed with himself for allowing himself to think of her provocatively he threw himself on the couch and stared at the ceiling. He ignored the alien sounds in his stomach before remembering that 'She' would also be hungry when she came back home, and sex would be at the top of her menu, not leftover dough.

Sipho clicked his tongue in frustration. He was getting himself worked up over something he had no control over. One thing he had control over, however, was what he could do to calm down. Without hesitation, he pulled out his phone and called his mother who answered on the third ring. It was almost a tradition, and any deviation would immediately ring alarm bells. "Hi Ma,"

"I hope you're calling me to tell me you've found the one."

"Not yet Ma,"

"Then why do you waste my airtime?"

"But I'm the one that always calls you," Sipho protested.

"Excuses, excuses, how are you, when are you coming to visit? We miss you,"

"Real soon, the term is almost over," Sipho smiled.

"Yes, and then my son will be some hotshot lawyer,"

"Ma, I'm not even studying law,"

"Well, I don't know. You guys have complicated things. Back in your Aunt's and my day, things were simple. Medicine, education, civil servant, those were your options and so that's what we became. Teachers and nurses, and then there's your Aunt who decided to be a Police officer. Thank God she didn't choose the army."

"Why did she join the police anyway, and not become a nurse like Aunt Judy?"

"You're asking me but day in and day out you sleep with her," Sipho's mother sighed.

Sipho shuffled uncomfortably as his mother continued to talk. He could picture her hand landing loudly on the side of her thigh from her throwing it in the air in over-exaggeration as he heard it in the background.

"Hey,"

"Yes Ma," he answered, hearing the word the third time around.

"I hope you're passing at school because you can't even pay attention when someone's talking to you."

"Sorry Ma," he said, running his hand behind the back of his head.

"Is everything okay though, my baby?"

Mother and child knew that by the time this question came along, their conversation was over, matter of fact, it was their way of saying goodbye to one another. Even though things weren't okay and Sipho wanted to just burst with emotion about what was going on but where would he begin? His culture hadn't equipped him with the skills to even begin approaching an adult when presented with such an issue. All he could do was say goodbye to his mother and continue with his life of seclusion with his Aunt.

3

Sipho felt it hard to breathe. His eyes blinded by bedroom lights forcing him to blink repeatedly before he felt the feeling that made it hard to breathe return. The second time around, it left soft kisses that tickled his skin, making it tingle as they made their way down his neck and under his chin.

"You like that don't you, big boy?" her voice was wet and husky as it filled Sipho's ear, causing him to shiver.

He tried to shove his Aunt off him but his hands were tied to each pillar of the bed and he lay there crucified, unable to do anything but wave his penis around as she continued to dot his body with kisses like a game of sudoku before she made her way south accompanied by a trail of manicured nails. He cried in distress when she massaged and dug them into his thighs.

Sipho growled.

"Relax, slow down. Wait for me," she whispered, her voice causing her nephew's nipples to sting in anticipation of hearing more of it. "I want to try something new and trust me when I say you'll enjoy it more than I will, I promise," unwrapping a condom with her teeth and winking at him.

Sipho's Adam's apple moved up and down as he swallowed hard, replacing the gesture that his head made. All his attention was now focused on dealing with his Aunt's weight as she cemented herself atop him before rocking back and forth.

"Wow, you're on fire today, aren't you? She panted before straddling him and grinding. She increased her pace until she could no longer keep up. Ignoring his intercourse between a moan and a scream when her own appendage left his dick with the sound reminiscent of a pool pump being pulled out of water. Although he refused to admit it, he enjoyed it even more so when she went from simply grinding to straddling him like a horse and began riding him. And when she quickened her pace, it drove him nuts. With each slap of her large rear against his tiny thighs it became as clear as day that he was about to impregnate her. Only to be left hanging at the zenith of ecstasy.

"What the fuck" Sipho screamed as he shot his semen into his latex pouch, completely missing the tight warm enclave offered by his Aunt.

"That's no way to talk to me," she said, slapping his cheek and continued to watch him fill up his condom like a burst water main, exchanging that sight for the look of anguish on his other head.

"All right, time to get you all cleaned up and ready for bed. Some of us have got work in the morning," she said, undoing the handcuffs.

Aunt Rebecca removed herself from Sipho's bed and disappeared from his room, leaving him to clean himself up, tired from the night's activities. He fell asleep immediately, but in the morning found it hard to wake up with his muscles stiff with pain. Now was the time for a massage, not yesterday. It was the perfect time to stop complaining and get on with life, but unfortunately, things didn't always go according to how one wanted them.

Mr Phewa was an efficient man when it came to teaching and it showed. At times, it felt like he was a student in a rush to get to his next class and so his lessons tended to have a habit of ending earlier than they should. This didn't matter much to Sipho, and he used the extra time to fetch his test papers. All was well, as he collected them all except for one. One test script he couldn't find but knew with certainty that he had written, submitted and it had come out because he had its contemporaries in his hand. He crawled around all the other scripts like a roach, paging through them one by one, diligently searching for his student number.

"If it's not there, then it's not here. Paging through them again won't make your script appear,"

Sipho stopped his frantic search, the voice directed his way startling him before continuing his search.

"Hey kid, I'm talking to you. Stop. I know how to do my job. The pile you're searching in now is third-year sociology, it's got nothing to do with you. That pile you couldn't stop digging in was first-year English,"

"Then where's my script?" Sipho asked with annoyance.

"The hell am I supposed to know, do I look like I keep track of every test paper that comes in here? Besides, what would make your paper so special to me that I should keep an eye out for it? Look, this university is a big place, see all those empty boxes?" The student asked, pointing at the hollow shelves behind Sipho. "All reserved for test papers, and so is this space here, now imagine finding one paper of a student who I don't know and probably failed in and amongst all those papers. See why I don't care?"

"So... what am I supposed to do now?"

"Part the red sea, build a crucifix, I don't know?" he shrugged, placing his feet on the table, and began playing with his phone. "Go to your lecturer and ask her why you don't have your script, tell her I sent you," waving him off.

"But who are you?"

"Don't worry, she knows who I am, I work here,"

Sipho turned around, his head sunk low, and did what he was told. He was halfway to where he was going when he realized that he was being made a fool of because he was a first year. How would his teacher know who the guy monitoring the test papers was? For all he knew, he was probably one of a few honours students trying to make some extra money, and a rude one at that. Instead of turning around and counting his losses, Sipho soldiered on. He'd play the first-year card and claim he didn't know protocols for lost scripts or make up some bullshit along those lines. Miss De Wet was busy and told him to come see her tomorrow after class and for following her instructions he was told to come back after an hour. He'd never make that hour because this time around it was he who had commitments and they were most definitely not meant for her. After class, it was the office, but she was busy. All he wanted was his test paper, something he wasn't even sure she had, but the lengths he was going to get it he wasn't even sure if it was worth it anymore. 15 minutes turned into 30 and 30 into 45, that's when throwing in the towel coincided with the end of De Wet's meeting.

"-Ya no, the kids are fine. Although between you and me, I sometimes wish they could disappear because it's always daddy this, daddy that," the man chuckled, causing Miss De Wet to chuckle politely with him.

"I completely understand Andreas, but they will grow up. It's a phase and it'll pass,"

"It can't come soon enough,"

Although Sipho wasn't the best when it came to relationships, even he could tell that this guy either had feelings or really wanted to be in Miss De Wet's pants.

"If you'll excuse me, I shouldn't keep Mr Bhengu waiting any longer than I have," Taking Sipho by surprise, but hearing his name from her mouth boded well for his missing script.

He slithered into her office, the man in jeans, a plaid shirt and a look from the depths of hell unflinching as they made eye contact on his way inside. He was visibly upset, all that was missing from this man was a toothpick, jeans, sunburn and a few more decades prior to the one they were in and Sipho would be calling Andreas 'Baas'.

"So," she began as she made her way to her desk, "how can I help you?"

"I was wondering if you know where I could find my script, I can't find it with the others and-"

"Here it is," she said, cutting him off mid-sentence.

Sipho looked at his paper and gave a satisfactory hum.

"I agree wholeheartedly with you in that department. I said the same thing while marking it," taking a sip out of her coffee mug.

Sipho paused, giving his script a look of contempt, as though he were drawing inspiration from it. "Miss De Wet, about last week. I'd like to -" he stopped, hoping that she'd stop him, but she just stared at him with her mug in hand. "I didn't mean to -" he could have stopped and left at any point in time. He'd obtained what he'd come for, but he couldn't, not yet anyway. He had this burning desire to continue, nobody forced him to, he knew perfectly well what he was doing. He tripped over his own words, but they soon found their feet as he continued to talk. "It's not that I can't talk, or that I won't talk, it's just that... I live with some powerful people and I don't want you to get hurt if I talk to you. I'm not even sure that this is safe as is,"

"Don't worry about me. I can handle myself if things are as dangerous as you say they are. It's your safety I'm more concerned about. Clearly, you're not in a position where you can pick up your things and just up and leave, be it physically, emotionally and financially, so just know my door is always open should you need to come vent out those frustrations," She smiled.

Sipho nodded and got off his stool, turned on his heel and headed for the door. He had just wasted his entire afternoon for nothing.

4

Conventional sex just wasn't doing it anymore for Aunt Rebecca. Sipho tried his best to provide her with the thrusts she needed to satisfy her sexual urges, but like a plastic bag of water with a hidden leak she just wouldn't fill up. Instead, it was he who suffered. It was he who had to endure her wet womanhood gliding up against his penis like an erotic slip and slide. Her vagina squeezing as it turned this way and that from one side to the next before letting go to do it all over again, feeling slipperier, needing for a tighter grip around Sipho. All he could do was stiffen powerlessly before digging his fingers into his palms. He didn't know what was worse, being tied up and not being able to use all your limbs during a climax or the satisfaction that came with the sensation of that very same orgasm stain your mother's sister's chest white. While she smiled enthusiastically back at him, ready to serve that viscous liquid like an entrée at her own private party.

No. that was no longer enough for Rebecca, who craved more out of her little sex toy despite him complaining about the pain in his pelvic region. She'd rubbed him with more than enough aloe vera to fix him. His inability to satisfy her despite all the training she had given him exhausted her, leaving her unsatisfied and forced to finish on her own. She didn't do it so he could fumble like a newly born baby goat.

"Ooh," he'd moan before filling up a condom.

Well, tonight she'd get her revenge. She squeaked as she walked, her feet clicking as the tips of her heels touched the ground. Saluting the squeaking they made on the tiled floor like the end of a poetry recital.

"You and Aunty are going to have some fun, aren't we?"

There was a shake of chains in protest, and Rebecca snapped her whip. Her subject sat blindfolded and chained to a chair with no seat, while Rebecca covered her dark skin with nothing but luminous pink latex. 'Shh, don't make me use this on you," she said, cracking her whip against the floor, clicking her heels across the cold tiles towards her nephew, who caused the chains to jingle in accordance with her approach. "Now we don't want that, now do we?" she whispered in the back of his ear, running the rubber down his naked body. She gently undid the gag on his mouth and told him that when she wanted her to stop, he should say yes. It was confusing, but she did so on purpose.

With the instructions related to him and his senses on high alert, all Sipho could do now was wait. The longer he waited the more tense his body became until he felt something touch his shoulder. He didn't know what it was, feather, ant, tip of a whip, or his Aunt's hand. "Yes!" he screamed.

'Okay, okay. No need to scream,"

Sipho couldn't believe it was that easy. If he'd known he would've asked his Aunt for a safe word a long time ago. He could hear what he assumed were her heels walking away. His body eased up and his shoulders relaxed, and it's only then that he realized just how much tension was in them. He heard his Aunt's footsteps return with a jingling of some sort and he thought this mess would finally be over. They tried this; it didn't work, they'd go back to the old stuff or better yet all of it would stop entirely. His surroundings became quiet. No keys, no heels, no talkative Aunt and before he had a chance to physically voice it out, her large frame was underneath him between his legs.

'If you shit on me or my floor, it'll be the last thing you ever do,"

Sipho was confused. All he felt was the familiarity of the penis pump until a searing sharp indescribable pain joined it. How could he not shit himself? It hurt so much, that's all he could focus on. How could this be a category on a porn site? How did gay men enjoy one another like this? These are the questions that ran through his mind as his Aunt raped him with a dildo. He wasn't even aware that she'd undone his chains and was now lying on the floor face down, ass up for his Aunt to enjoy unhindered. What was she doing? Why was she taking her time and why wasn't things hurting anymore? Had it made his ass numb? Sipho was awash with questions in the darkness and the more he waited for her to do something or more of the same, the more she'd flip the script and do something different.

Sipho skipped school for the day and was told to stop exaggerating how much pain he was in and head to school the next day. But he didn't attend any lectures or fetch any papers, but quietly make his way to Miss De Wet's office. If she was one of his Aunt's spies, then to hell with it. She seemed like a nice person to rat him out, and if it came down to it and she did double-cross him, he only had himself to blame. He stood blockaded by that big brown door with her name on it like the bouncer to the VIP section of an elite club. He knocked hard and knocked fast and immediately prayed that she wasn't there.

"Come in," sang a voice from the other side.

Sipho found it hard to breathe as if his Aunt were on top of him. His hand shook as he bit into his nails nervously. He swore under his breath and closed his eyes.

"Come in?"

With one hand on the door handle and the other ready to turn around and run away, the only thing that filled Sipho's mind was the sound of his heart galloping like a herd of buffalo. "Ah, fuck it," he whispered, biting his bottom lip and tore open the door and past Miss De Wet who had stood up to go answer the door herself.

"Mr Bhengu, what a lovely sur-"

"My Aunt is forcing me to sleep with her," sitting on the table before turning to face her.

5

Sipho wasn't ready to go home not because friends were few but for whatever reason could be put up for debate as a good one. He was confused about whether to clench or relax as both actions hurt but doing nothing hurt more, what hurt him the most was the pain that came with not being able to tell anybody about it. With his tears counted as he washed his face and started his day. He had several missed calls from his Aunt which he chose to ignore, but she had sent a few useful messages that had nothing to do with sex. His day wouldn't seem to come to an end, not only would he have to catch up from all the days he'd missed from school, but because he didn't have his books, he'd still be left behind and it was infuriating. At home, he sought to catch up, but it was all too much. If he was battling with first-year, how was he going to make it to the third year, was he even going to pass the year, let alone get his degree? All the philosophical questions came to a halt when the sound of a door slam and keys sliding on the kitchen table filled the house. Sipho would've held his breath and tense up but it was just too painful. So he settled for a whatever happens, happens, mental approach and continued on with his schoolwork.

Sure enough, his Aunt and he crossed paths when she walked past his room and saw a faint light coming from under the door. With a knock on the door, she was inside before he had a chance to reply.

"Awu, you're back?" she asked, genuinely surprised.

"Yes, Aunty."

"Why didn't you say so? All this time I'm here thinking I'm alone when I've got company,"

"Sorry,"

"And my calls? Why didn't you answer them to let me know you're not coming back?" she said, speaking to his reflection in the dresser.

"Sorry, my battery died," he lied, looking back at her through his dresser. She stood at the doorway for what seemed to be a long time before she disappeared. Even if she came back with a whip and beat her or rope and choked him to death, Sipho didn't care anymore, what his Aunt had done to him had ruined him forever. What's worse was, what she had done to him was in the dark so whenever he closed his eyes, he got a glimpse of her torturous ways. When he was in poorly lit areas, it reminded him of it and when it was time for bed. It stayed with him throughout the night.

The weeks that followed were like any other family, Aunt Rebecca went to work and Sipho went to school. The only difference was that he spent more time with Miss De Wet than with all her other students combined. Not that anybody cared but word started going around that Miss De Wet and Sipho were sleeping together. Sipho being who he was, was, of course, oblivious to what was going on due to his personal problems. For starters, he still felt guilty for being unable to please his Aunt sexually, even if it hurt in more ways than one. For any normal person, this shouldn't have bothered them, in fact, the news should've been cause for celebration as it gave them a way out, a reason for their abuser to discard them because they weren't of any interest to them anymore. But for Sipho, his guilt extended much deeper than that. It was his fault he couldn't please his Aunt, even if he didn't want it with everything in his body. This was no way to repay the person who gave him everything he wanted, needed, for free when others paid for it. A place to sleep, eat, WiFi, all these necessities were for free in exchange for 2 hours of pleasure because she was too busy to go look for a sexual partner and he couldn't even do that. It was extremely selfish of him on his part and it was time to change that, even if it was once. Just once, and hopefully, she'd leave him alone. On the flip side, was the possibility that she would come back for more, a mosquito in the night, unseen but heard, but it was a gamble he was prepared to take.

"Sipho?"

"Hmm?" he hummed, his attention returning to the present.

"Are you sure you don't want to talk about what's troubling you? I know it can't be easy to open up about being sexually abused by someone you love and trust. And whatever happens, please don't ever think for a second that because of your gender, it makes it any less right? Sexual abuse is sexual abuse regardless of whether you're male, female, cat or dog. Please understand that,"

Sipho nodded silently.

"And I'm sorry."

"For?" Sipho asked, confused.

"I promised myself I wouldn't get preachy no matter what happens, but I couldn't stop myself. It just came out, so I'd like to apologize."

"It's okay," Sipho smiled. "I know you mean well."

"Look. I'm not going to mother you, nor force you to talk to me, you're all grown up and if you want to come here and stare at the walls that's fine but you have to let me know so I can get some work while you do it. I can't stare at you do it. Unfortunately, I know this sounds harsh but the whole point of me allowing you to come here was for you to talk about your Aunt and what she's doing to you if you don't feel ready to report her because keeping it inside is not the right course of action. And yet, you've decided to proceed with that very action which I was hoping you'd avoid, for the past few weeks you haven't said much. Besides you no longer want to stay in that house, but you have nowhere else to go."

"I can't because she's a Major in the police."

"Oh, that does provide a bit of a technical problem, doesn't it?"

"Yes. And if I'm going to report her it means having to go to another province, like the North West or Northern Cape, because all the police stations here are going to report back to her and let her know." Sipho explained to her before she even proposed the question.

"And how do you know this?"

"Because I live with her, she's told me this several times. I've tried to call her bluff on it by reporting a phone stolen in the most remote police station I could find on the outskirts of Free State in Ladybrand and she still found out about it,"

"How did you get that far?"

"A friend of mine who got a car for her birthday. But she doesn't talk to me now," He shrugged.

"So your next best plan is to go out of the province and report her?"

"That won't work either, because I'll just be told to report the crime in the province in which it happened like a sane person would do. You can't have your car stolen in Cape Town and then go report it in Durban, what are they supposed to do?"

Miss De Wet was stumped. She wanted to help, but she didn't know where to begin. She wanted to honour her word of not saying anything, but who was she going to report her to if she held such a prominent position in the justice system?

6

It was a random, unsuspecting night when an uncomfortable but familiar weight pressed up against his body that stirred him awake. He attempted to leave but found that he was bound and gagged to the pillars of his bed as they shook against the wall. "Shh, you'll wake up the neighbours," came a whisper. An order with the use of a manicured finger that landed on his restrained mouth. At least this time he could be thankful that he had the power of sight, so he could prepare for his torture before it arrived. As his assailant eased off him, relieving the pressure from his body as she stood at the foot of his bed in nothing but what was, in essence, a strip of tight leather across her chocolate chest and hot pants that disappeared into nothingness as she gave him a tour of her outfit.

"You like?" Catching her nephew staring at her in lust, his beady little eyes making her feel objectified, but that same feeling turning her on. She placed her hands around her waist revealing more of her full figure as she thought of what to do next, things weren't going as she had planned, but she was enjoying the attention. How could she not when Sipho's bulge began to grow? Constricting his thigh, a python passing over a springbok on its side causing her to inevitably bite her bottom lip, her nipples becoming knobs on a gas stove and doing what they were designed to below.

Sipho caught himself nodding to her question, but he didn't care. His attention was more focused on her superhero pose and how the black leather seemed to stretch around her breasts without flying off and more amazing still, the way it stuck to her body, capturing its shape, flaws and all. The leather was sellotaped on tight, too tight, and it began to make sense why the back of what was meant to be hot pants merely vanished into nothingness when they made it past her thighs. And when she stood there with her hands on her hips like a sexy superhero, nothing shone brighter than the contours of her womanhood. Imprisoned in leather like the rendering from an artist, it held back all those juices, baking them inside his mental gas stove. He was in pain just thinking about it and how wet they were making her, preventing her from sliding up and down his cock. What's worse was how he was unable to adjust his dick and it drove him wild. It made him restless, and his legs shook, making him throw a tantrum since that's all he could do.

"Is this what you what?" his Aunt asked, rubbing her camel toe to spirited agreement. Sipho's enthusiasm made her moist and her nipples even harder, but her horniness had nowhere to go, making it all the more blindsiding. She crept up on the bed like a leopard, brushing up against the bulge that had grown to its full length and caused him to purr unbearably through his gag.

"Oops," she grinned before removing it to kiss him. Even though he was bound and unable to move his arms. It was she who was getting a lesson on how to use her tongue, their mouths met and his tongue slipped into her waiting mouth. Not to be outdone by a child, she finally let her interior breath and then set about teaching Sipho the art of pleasing a woman using his tongue. Everything was just for show, petals on a flower and the only thing he should focus on was the centre where the pollen was, and being the astute student he was Sipho focused on the clitoris and nothing else and it took no time at all for his Aunt's knees to buckle while he continued to devour her like a cannibal until she didn't have the strength to stand.

Sipho knew that with his Aunt's ass in the air shaped like the back of a drumstick, all he had to do was play white noise and ignore the slurping that came with it or else he'd choke her throat with his glue.

She held on to his nuts like lucky dice as she swallowed him whole. "Stop," Sipho groaned out of breath, throwing his legs in the air in an effort to get her to stop.

"Sorry, that's not the safe word," she said as a disclaimer, her mouth making a popping sound.

"Shit"

"Yes," his mind returned to him only to be ignored by his elder.

She continued to vacuum him, tentative at first but growing with confidence as her strokes became more aggressive, matching her nephew's wails of pleasure, mixed with discomfort until she thought he'd had enough before performing her magnum opus. Without giving him time to recover she was already in her favourite position, with her head hidden behind her large ass she began teasing him, dipping the tip of his head into her glistening unzipped slit, listening to him agonize about how much he wanted to slap her fat ass, making her even wetter, which could only make things worse for him. Even though she did this for what was merely seconds, it must have felt like hours on his part because she'd never heard a man so happy to feel a wet and moist vagina lubricate his throbbing cock. And as she fucked him, the back of her combed head appearing and then disappearing as her soft skin clapped against his thighs, she could feel herself quiver over his inexperienced flesh. The harder she jumped on him, the louder she became, tuning her clitoris in the process until she felt her legs shake. She had one of two choices, pull out now or fuck the shit out of this dick and come all over it? It was the best god damn orgasm she had had in a while. Ya no, this wasn't a porn movie or a Jane Austen novel. The reality was, however, she'd had good sex, not the quietest but what could she say, the dick was good and she was still riding it until she felt it was enough, before lying beside her nephew, winded.

She didn't say anything, nor did he, after all, this was merely sex, not a date. Once the heavy breathing was over and what seemed to be a decent amount of time had passed, Sipho felt a smooth, subtle feeling brush up against his thigh. He tried his best not to give his Aunt the satisfaction of another round, but here she was, doing what she had to, to peel him open like a banana. She had her legs folded like chicken wings and swung her ass back and forth in his face, before illustrating all the unique positions a woman could enjoy while a male was chained to a bed. It didn't take long though, as her manicured fingers hung onto his shoulders for support while she beat him like an egg for her to feel the familiar stiffness and breath-holding that came from Sipho before he came. She continued to ride him. She slipped and skidded all over the place, and he was just dealing with it. His load was warm and it went deep. A part of her wished she'd unwrapped him beforehand so he could grab her by the waist and push it deeper inside her, but what was done was done. She sat up once Sipho had stopped panting. "You enjoyed that, didn't you?" tapping him on the nose.

"Yes,"

"Guess leather is dangerous for both of us," Rebecca gasped, sliding off him. She removed his restraints before picking up her garments and disappearing to go take a shower. She was still taken aback by how different things were this time around. His nods and moans seemed like those of enjoyment and not of those of fear she was so accustomed to. Meanwhile, for Sipho, the penny dropped at what had just happened.

7

It seemed like Sipho's plan had worked, his Aunt's requests for sex had decreased dramatically if not disappeared entirely since their last encounter, but it came at a cost. He enjoyed parts of it, not all of it. Even though he couldn't bring himself up to admit it or face the truth. It destroyed him, but with everything looking so misaligned, there was hopefully one person who could rearrange them, assuming his navigational assumptions were correct in the first place. A phone call out towards them was answered after the signature three rings. The phone clicked and the voice that soothed him immediately spoke on the other end.

"Ma,"

"Sipho. This is a surprise, is everything okay?"

They had their usual banter of irrelevant conversation before Sipho got down to his reason for calling.

"I need you, please come,"

His mother laughed. "You think this is a movie where everybody can just drop down whatever they're doing and go, neh?"

"Please, it's important?"

"Why can't you ask your Aunt, she's a police officer. Maybe you can even get her to shoot them while she's at it?" Sipho's mother chuckled at her own joke.

"Please Ma, I'll even pay for your bus. It's about her,"

"Tell me what's wrong then, my baby?"

"Ma please, I haven't seen you in so long, please... even if it's for a day, a weekend," Sipho cried, unable to hold himself.

"Okay, don't cry my baby. Mommy's coming, okay,"

"Okay," Sipho sniffed. "I love you,"

"I love you too,"

Sipho put the razor down and untied the rope, slowing down blood flow to make the vein in his wrist look bigger. The next day started off on jagged footing, the makeup he was using to cover up the bruising left behind by being tied up had run out and he'd forgotten to replace it. It was a hot day, so wearing a hoodie or sweatshirt wouldn't make any sense whatsoever. The only saving grace he had wasn't the fact that it was Friday and his mother was coming. Besides a few looks here and there, all was going well, this wasn't high school where people would tease you for your clothing choices. However, he did regret it and boy did the Free State sun make sure he knew it. The key, however, was to stay hydrated as much as possible and not let whatever makeup he had left get smeared off by his sweatshirt, but as the day wore on that simple task became more of an unattainable challenge. One lecture down and two to go. The great idea of keeping cool in the computer labs hit him way too late and soon it was time for English. His greatest obstacle as it was a venue with virtually no ventilation. But there he was, sitting as close as he could to the door to obtain whatever cough of a breeze passed by. The lecture ended, he gave it a mental fist bump and that's the last thing he could remember.

To everybody else around him, however, the lecture ended and they all shuffled out the stuffy venue, a herd of wildebeest to the watering hole that was the tiny entrances in which they had come in at the beginning of the lecture. They descended and made their way out only to be hindered in the process by a fainting strangler. Others jumped over it, not caring and the majority avoided the dead carcass in a heated effort not to get sucked in by Miss De Wet's efforts to remove it from her class. As they helped Sipho, hoisting him up, they began their journey towards the infirmary.

"No, take him to my office,"

The two male students looked at each other in confusion but said nothing, obeying their lectures' commands. It made no sense since the infirmary was closer but to the office, they trotted, dumping Sipho there before disappearing, never to be seen again until the next English lesson. The first thing she did was cool the place down and remove his sweatshirt, and it revealed the rings, his smeared makeup that he'd tried to cover up. She removed him from the floor and placed him on a chair before waking him up gently. "Sipho," she spoke to him calmly.

The first thing he did when his eyes shot open and realized he wasn't wearing his sweatshirt was stare at his wrists, they were covered in makeup and the blending that was far superior to how he'd learnt how to do so. He looked up at his surroundings and found he was in Miss De Wet's office and a glass of water waiting for him. She was busy with some work, oblivious to his presence. He drank the water gingerly, not sure what he should do next before returning to his wrists as if he had recently rediscovered them after losing them for a long time. He looked up from them to find her staring at him.

"Keeping hydrated and staying in a cool dry place can only take you so far,"

"You're not going to ask about my wrists?"

"Why, we all have them?" Miss De Wet answered. "But if you insist, are the bruises from your Aunt?"

"She handcuffs me to the bed before she does bad things to me,"

"You mean sex?" De Wet asked for clarification to ensure she wasn't assuming.

Sipho nodded, bowing his head.

"I think it's time to go to the professionals about this, I know what we said in the beginning but this isn't working. We can't go to the police, so how's about Childline as a Plan B?"

"Wait, I thought you said you were a professional psychologist?"

"You've just suffered from heatstroke, there's still a bit of disorientation. What I said is that I could help. The only profession I have is this one, I'm afraid. But listen to me Siph-"

"No. You told me you were a psychologist, that's why I trusted you. That's why I told you... told you this. You lied to me!"

"Sipho, please sit down. I can see why you're visibly upset, but there's a logical explanation for this,"

"No," Sipho shouted.

Miss De Wet moved from her side of the table to the other side where Sipho stood firm with fists clenched on either side of his body, averting eye contact.

"Is this why you've been quiet for the past several weeks?"

At first, her question was ignored, but her company moved his head forward. She didn't need to know about what his Aunt had done to his ass nor how much he missed her having sex with him now that she'd stopped. Still, he did need help in getting her to stop completely or better still, getting away from her. She approached him with intent, wiping away the tears spray-painted on his cheeks and wrapped her arms tightly around him, but her betrayal of his trust didn't allow him to reciprocate her gesture of compassion.

Without warning, Andreas splattered in, left to see and interpret things however he saw fit. His eyes danced up and down as he saw his Jolene and this black boy that proved to be a thorn in his side before him. And he was here to confirm it, with his own eyes.

"Jolene?" his voice, before repeating her name, his voice with much more bravado the second time around.

"Knocking is a foreign concept to you?" she asked

"What is this?" he asked, changing from English to Afrikaans as he spoke.

They exchanged a few heated questions before Jolene asked what he wanted. Too angry to answer, Andreas left and so too had Sipho in the commotion.

8

Sipho felt like a four-year-old. He wanted his mother, and he wanted his mother now. However, he was surprised to find her and her sister home before him as he wanted to prepare some sort of surprise before she got there. Instead, Sipho returned home to one of, if not the warmest reception ever from school. He had begged his mother to come, and she'd finally arrived only for her presence to startle him. Even his Aunt arrived early from work to keep up the appearance of a happy family as she watched with envy a mother smush and choke her child with hugs upon seeing him. His slender frame pressed up against his heavyset mother like a child. Nothing made Sipho happier, literally, every burden that he carried with him diffused itself onto her and for those brief moments, he was in heaven.

"Hi Ma, "he said with a toothy smile.

"Do you come home from school this late every day?"

"Not always, but most of the time?" he shrugged.

"Well, which one is it, not always or most of the time, it can't be both?" crossing her arms across her chest.

"Uh?"

"Well, it better be worth it. It's time for you to finish at this university, get a job and bring home a wife,"

"But I just started?" Sipho protested, confused.

"Excuses, excuses. No funny business, just books. I will not be looking after any babies, I'm letting you know now. You'll drop out of this waste of money now and do it yourself,"

"Ma," Sipho shouted.

"Don't shout at me. Who do you think you're talking to?"

"No Ma, I'm not having sex," he answered, looking at his Aunt.

"Good. Keep it that way,"

This is what Sipho wanted. This is why he wanted his mother here. His mother had agreed to visit, convincing her aside, he had no reason to complain but he was already getting tired of having her around and she hadn't asked for him to make her a cup of tea yet. Yet her presence was essential. He could finally sleep without fear, yet he still woke up to check if he was still chained.

He was scared, make no mistake about that. A plethora of what-if scenarios overflowed through his mind every time he lay his head on the couch, but the one saving grace in his possession was his acute sense of hearing. He could tell who went to the toilet at night by their footsteps. But he could never hear his Aunt leave for work, nor when she was in the kitchen and she only gave herself away when doing one of three things, placing something in the sink, grabbing her keys or closing the door.

"I still don't know why you people call this place the Tourism Centre, there's nothing that attracts tourists to this city. Worst of all, you put it behind a stadium."

Rebecca sighed, she knew this was bound to happen, it was only a matter of time before Palesa started complaining. She never saw the good in anything, always the bad, no matter what it was. As religious as she was, Jesus could come back tomorrow and she'd find something bad to say despite going to church every Sunday and praying for him to return and do good. "He probably had a fight with God, blah, blah, or something along those lines." This was Palesa, after all. But she didn't blame her, partly. The better part of their life was spent being raised by a single father and Rebecca had to act as a single mother from time to time to fill in the essential stepping stones that their father couldn't such as teaching her how periods work.

While Palesa was tearing apart Rebecca's home decor, despite her giving her a sizable amount of money at the end of the month to live off of and accommodate her son so he could finish school. Miss De Wet was in her office with a bottle of vodka on her table. A gift from a friend who was no more and used the bottle as a means to remember her. She had her signature mug to her lips and took calculated sips out of it while she thought of what took place earlier today and how she would have handled it better. She found it useful to take time to reflect on the day's events, no matter what happened. Her bottle of vodka served as a companion to her thoughts back to Andreas's outlandish behaviour after he barged into her office. But before she could decide what to do with that fool, she needed to be honest with herself and decide what she was going to do with Sipho. What was her intention? It was obvious the boy was in trouble and the deeper she dived into his pain the harder she found it to get out. She had to choose if she would embrace his story, feel his pain and tell it, or back away now. Which was it going to be? She flared her nostrils before placing her lips back on her mug. She remembered how all her questions were ignored until she asked him if this was why he'd been quiet for the past several weeks. It was a standard question of interest, but it seemed to be the straw that broke the camel's back. Watching someone cry was always an emotional experience, but knowing the difference in the types of emotional reactions is what made all the difference between my condolences and physical contact. The greatest of pains were the ones that were never spoken of nor shared because they were the ones that were too much to bear. But expressed visually with nothing more than inconspicuous tears. Miss De Wet, who had experience in that particular field recognised them instinctively and wrapped Sipho inside her arms, allowing him to tsk unabashed... until he blundered in.

"Jolene?" an angry voice boomed from the door, swiftly untying their embrace.

"Knocking a foreign concept to you?" She asked.

"What's going on here?"

"Come again?"

"What is this, what are you doing?" he demanded.

"Come again?"

"Are you going to answer me or are you going to keep repeating the word come again?"

Jolene was speechless, taking a moment to collect her thoughts while her colleague demanded answers. Making her seem guilty of something in the process. "Where the hell do you get off asking me what's going on, in my office, no less?" She yelled.

The two exchanged heated words in Afrikaans before Jolene conceded. "What do you want?" She incurred with a defeated spirit.

"What?" Andreas asked, thrown off by her question.

"Don't 'what' me. What did you want, coming to my office and demanding answers from me like a child? Why are you here, Andreas?"

"What, was I disturbing you from something... because you two seemed really cosy when I walked in?" Andreas snapped with an upper body covered in pink skin.

"And that's the problem. You walk in here and make assumptions and demand things based on throwing shit at the fan and seeing what sticks. You haven't said anything newsworthy and even if you did, you could've just as easily emailed whatever it is you were bringing, which you still haven't told me what it is, if you had anything, to begin with?" Jolene gave a fake smile.

Andreas clenched his jaw and squinted at her.

"Problem?"

He hummed what could be interpreted as a no out of his stiff body.

"You work in Human Resources, right? Well, I assume, so I'm still trying to figure out what you're doing in my office and why you won't tell me why are you here in my office?"

"Yes, you're right, I do work in Human Resources," speaking for the first time after a long while. "And I'll tell you why I'm here. Teacher-student relations are not allowed, he said confidently as he crossed his arms and towered over Jolene.

"And what proof do you have of this?"

"I saw enough," he dismissed. "You know Jolene; I didn't want to believe it. I gave you the benefit of the doubt, I said no, not Jolene, she wouldn't. She couldn't, yet... I saw it with my own eyes," he said soothingly.

"But if you're going to start investigating lecture-student relationships, there're plenty of guilty culprits and at the top of that list is Johan. You and I both know this, so why come after me?"

"So you do admit that you're having one?" Andreas pointed at her accusingly.

Jolene sighed and ran her hand through her hair, taking a step back. She was defending herself against a man who acted like a jealous boyfriend and the worst part was that he couldn't even fire her even if she had done something wrong. "Have I done something wrong to you because I can't seem to figure out where all this anger comes from?"

"Yes. It's because this of... this thing you have going on with little black boys is wrong Jolene. All you have to do is open your eyes and look at what's in front of you in order for you to be truly happy. I don't know what or who is leading you astray, but you're going to pay for it."

"And who are you to decide, God? Matter of fact, get out of my office." She demanded, pushing him out.

He obliged allowing himself to be manhandled out by her, as short as she was compared to him. "Just thought I should tell you, I know people who work in finances?" He said, spiralling around once at the doorway.

"Meaning?" she asked, shooting him a quizzical look.

"I can make things could happen," he shrugged.

"So what, on top of trying to get me fired you're going to stop paying me?" she laughed. "Nice try. Go try that bullshit on someone else,"

"Just because I don't work in finance doesn't mean I can't talk to someone who can? Oh and as for trying my stunt on someone else, I have,"

"What do you mean?"

"Just because you know I can't fire you doesn't mean everybody you were romantically involved with does," Andreas shrugged before leaving her office.

It took a while for Jolene to register who he was referring to and she realised what he was talking about. Although Andreas had been an obnoxious douche, she'd often go out with him on lunch dates and put up with him just to stop him from pestering her, she'd never pictured him to be such an evil man. It made sense why so many women were against men now that she'd experienced it herself despite men having done far worse, she agreed, men were seriously trash.

9

Sipho washed dishes in silence, it was mid-afternoon and the activity was quite soothing. Not only was it the right thing to do, but he had to do it while his mother was still gallivanting. You know, keep the kitchen sink clean, pick up after himself and a whole host of other things that they'd agreed upon before he left home to come live with his Aunt. So while she was here, he'd have to do it and Vannessa would take some days off, only fluttering for laundry. He decided then and there that he was going to clean the pots in the evening and nobody was going to tell him otherwise, without warning his mother joined in and began helping him in silence taking on the task of wiping anything which was already on the dishrack. Sipho had it in him to ask his mother what she was doing but he didn't want to ruin the rare moment in fear that she might use his interest as a reason to stop. All she did was wipe and neatly categorize them to make it easier for her to put them away where they belonged, because she didn't know where they stayed or simply didn't want to.

"I'm glad your Aunt has found someone," Palesa said as soon as her son grabbed the first lot of the dry dishes to put away.

"Ma,"

"I said, I'm glad your Aunt found someone,"

"Ah Ma, isn't this a conversation you should have with Aunt B?"

"Ayi man Sipho, you're older now. I'm sure you're mature enough to handle this. Besides, I've told you much worse things than thinking that Rebecca is dating again,"

"Yes, Ma," Sipho nodded. "So what makes you think she's dating again?"

"Don't tell her I told you this," she whispered, despite it being just the pair of them in the house. "But I found a pair of sexy clothes and a whip, for what, I don't know? But the clothes I'm sure are to charm someone," Sipho watched as her mother spoke with a glint in her eye, assuming that she wanted to trade places wasn't far off and no one would blame Sipho for the assumption. "Let's hope so," he lied, knowing very well what that 'sexy dress' and whip were for.

"Let's hope so indeed, and pray we meet this mystery man,"

Sipho found it hard to swallow but he forced himself to ask the next question. "Why?"

"Because Rebecca is too much. Yes, we get it, she's smart and independent but sometimes she just takes things to the extreme. She needs to let go of the past so she can heal. Make me a cup of tea," she said, grabbing a chair and sitting down in the tiny dining room. "You know Sipho, I've tried my very best to do all I can do for you as a mother and I can say I've done well to give you the best,"

Sipho nodded in agreement.

Palesa kept quiet for a long time. "So has your Aunt," she sniffed. "She's been more than just a sister to me,"

The memories of what she was thinking of began to overwhelm her. She'd even lay waste to the fact that she was speaking to a child as she pulled a crumpled tissue out of her chest. She just wanted to offload what was bothering her. "Rebecca's been through a lot and she's come a long way, but she's still got a long way to go. The problem with her is that she bottles everything up, that's her biggest problem," Paleasa thought as she accepted her tea.

Sipho listened in silence, unmoving as if he were a gecko plastered on the wall. He had mastered the habit of being invisible in the presence of others. Whatever was eating his mom was probably eating her just as much, if not more, as whatever was eating him, her uncontrolled outburst of attention and acknowledgement to the wrong person a telltale sign of the longer the pain was left unspoken the more it hurt.

"But I don't blame her. Ever since mom died things became tough. She doesn't think I know, but I know what dad did to her," thinking out loud more than anything. "I used to pretend I was asleep and listen to the grunts, moans and pained squeaks that used to come from that un-plastered roof of a house. I never thought she'd find happiness or a man due to my misandristic mentality. Maybe she's fallen in love with a woman and she's a lesbian, who am I to judge?"

He may have been young, but that didn't mean he didn't know what genuine pain felt like. If he could, he would've told his mother to shut up and told her about the real reason he wanted her to visit, the fact that he wanted her around because he was scared of her sister. How every time, if the wind blew too hard at night and caused his bedroom door to rattle it would startle him awake, ending any chance of going back to sleep. How he liked being fucked with a dildo in his ass and he didn't know whether it made him gay or not? And these were just the problems that happened in this house with the person who so-called-raised her. How was he supposed to tell her about the warnings from school he didn't know how to explain because he didn't know what they were for? All he could do though was take charge of what was in his control, hide his demons and smile, pretending like everything was okay. Everybody seemed so angry and for no reason but sort of made sense now. Who was he kidding, none of it made sense, his family was just fucked up, nothing more but good material for a book or a documentary?

As the semester rolled up its sleeves preparing for the final push before it closed, things changed between English lecturer and student. The student stopped coming to her class entirely despite submitting his test papers and passing them. This was an exceptional feat of mental strength on the student's part, but the lecturer didn't like this one bit and failed him, for no particular reason. Sipho was beside himself but involving the right authorities to fix the issue put him at ease, especially because it meant that he qualified to write his final year exams. The disadvantage was that it reunited the student and teacher with one another. After Miss

De Wet had been reprimanded, she took advantage of the situation since she finally had Sipho's attention, granted he didn't want anything to do with her, understandably so, but she had made up her mind and if she was going to sever ties with him like this relationship was headed, then there were things he needed to know.

Sipho was overwhelmed by everything that was happening around him and pretending that everything was okay began to slip through his hands like fine sand. There was a feeling of helplessness and failure, worst of all, it was during his mother's visit. The one person he wanted to make proud of more than anybody else. He wanted protection from his Aunt, but instead, he got gossip and ranting. Of course, all this was done with the scent of liquor stuck to her breath so that was good to know, but that Sipho had no prior knowledge that mother drank in the first place was disconcerting. If she could harbour such a secret while spilling out so many, what else was she hiding? Or had the affinity for alcohol been something new? A sign that there was something wrong at home? But these were just the problems that had developed overnight with the person in front of him and he'd omitted the problems he had with the individual under whose roof they lived under.

Later on that evening in the depths of the night, Rebecca switched off the TV, startling Sipho awake. She waited for him to be conscious before she proceeded with her ballsy visit in the middle of the night. Was his Aunt going to do this here, now? Sipho's chest constricted despite having a functional set of lungs, his shortness of breath indescribable and unable to catch the next breath to voice it out. He'd never felt like this before, this feeling was new and a small voice at the back of his mind told him to scream for his mother, that's why she was here in the first place. The only other adult in the house who could help was right beside him but all she did was stare at him and watch him suffer, which felt worse than having her stroke his leg, increasing the heightened sensation of lust even though they might get caught. But no, she sat there, as though she were staring at a piece of art she was contemplating on buying. Although he started trembling, Sipho couldn't feel it. Even though Rebecca started this, she left, leaving her nephew to suffer from dizziness and panting.

"Here," she said, handing him a glass of water and helping him sit up.

Sipho obeyed the instruction without hesitation, drinking the water gingerly and setting the glass aside once he thought he was okay. Silence filled the dim lounge, as there was no TV to offer a distraction. The only light came from the kitchen and the passage, lighting up faces of confusion and apathy. Sipho shifted uncomfortably as he waited for something to happen and when it did, he flinched, causing his Aunt to pause before she continued and dug into the pockets of her gown and pulled out an envelope.

"What's this?"

"Ah, shit," he sighed.

"So you're not even going to bother to explain this?"

"What's there to explain, it's pretty straightforward. It's a disciplinary warning," Sipho shrugged.

Although Rebecca was irked by the way her nephew addressed her, lacking the level of respect she expected from him, it was a clear indication of something wrong. "Why do you have one because you're not the type of person to stir up trouble, skip classes or start revolutions unless I'm wrong, please correct me?"

"It doesn't matter," he mumbled.

"Oh no, it does. How else were you going to attend this hearing alone? Hire or pay people to be your family? It doesn't work that way. How are we meant to help you if you won't even tell us what's wrong?"

"If the problem is one of your teachers, I can go over there and talk to them?"

"No!" Sipho barked. "I mean no, that's not it, nor necessary," Sipho sighed, drowning in his hands as he looked at his Aunt's irritated gaze. He didn't even know where to begin, how much of the truth did she deserve to know or whether she was prepared for it at all?

10

Mr Bhengu avoided Ms De Wet as much as humanly possible, a clear indication of the power of words and the effect they had over people, but Ms De Wet being the type of person that she was, pursued him in the same manner a dog at customs looks for drugs. Sipho's schooling safety was at risk, but something Ms De Wet didn't have to consider. He sat in her office nervously, his body twitchy as he focused his attention on things he never paid attention to before while he was in here before, the type of books, pottery, art, and flora she possessed.

"Have you ever wondered why I stopped you that day at the end of class?" She asked without looking up from her work.

"No," Sipho said, thinking whether he wanted to know. "Why?" he continued.

"Oh, you know the usual, low self-esteem, hung shoulders, arms with signs of you cutting yourself,"

Sipho pulled down his hoodie to hide his wrist, even though there was nothing to hide at this point. "So the reason you haven't reported me is that I'm just some charity case to you. Some poor black kid you used to make yourself feel good about yourself and convince yourself you've made the world a better place so you can sleep better at night. You're nothing but a fraud, wasting students' time with pointless information,"

"Wait, what? Sipho, please sit down,"

"No. I'm tired of being your little pet project, your entertainment of sexual abuse because Netflix and TLC don't give you your fix,"

Ms De Wet sighed, which seemed to make Sipho even angrier. She remained absent in her words, almost as though her voice added fuel to the flame that was burning before her, and boy was Sipho on fire.

"You know what? You sit here and talk shit about me finding a voice, opening up, and finding the strength to go to the police. You want me to find my voice, well here it is. Fuck you, Jolene. Fuck you Jolene De Wet," He said, slamming the table. "Fuck you and this holier than though advice teaching you think you're giving and the fact that you're failing me in your class," Pointing at her before turning on his heel and disappearing behind the door, slamming it behind him.

"That went well," she said to herself after a moment, placing an end to the silence that weighed down her office.

The door flung open and the cavity it created Sipho barged in, startling her. "I forgot my textbook," he grumbled, trying to maintain the same level of gusto he had left with.

"Sipho listen," Jolene's voice was hard and stern, just like her grip on the child's arm as he failed to pull it away causing fear to dance in his eyes.

"Sit,"

Without hesitation, he slowly sat down, doing so in a way that reminded him of his Aunt causing fear and lust to course through his body concurrently but he ignored it to appear like a normal human being. He felt vulnerable and wondered whether she'd take advantage of him as her primary caregiver was doing. Even if she were to, he was a sitting duck, the whole university already thought it was happening he was being given disciplinary warnings because of it even though he hadn't even given his penis more than two shakes at the bathrooms and worst of all, if she were to do it, she had all the information on how to replicate or build upon her Aunt's methods and make them better, if such a thing were even possible. What could stop her? She could continue her streak to fail him if he refused to do something she wanted. If he did get expelled, how would he explain this at home, they'd obviously believe the school over him, regardless of who was right or wrong. What would his Aunt say, no, what would she think, let alone do to him if she knew he allowed someone else other than her to do to him what she was the only person allowed to?" It was all too much, the questions wouldn't stop. It was just -

"Sipho" Miss De Wet snapped her fingers repeatedly while repeating his name. "I need you here with me. What I'm about to tell you is..." She took a deep breath.

While Sipho had blacked out due to his multitude of questions, his lecturer leaned on her desk to face him with his textbook in her hand. "Let's start from the top, with why I stopped you that day. Because you have low self-esteem and exhibit signs of suicidal behaviour. How do I know this?" she asked, playing with the pages of Sipho's textbook. "Because I learned how to recognize them. What I didn't expect nor was I prepared for in any way, shape or form was the reasons behind those failed attempts at suicide. I wish I could say I can imagine what you're going through, to have your body do the opposite of what you tell it to, making the one who tortures you believe that you enjoy what they're doing to you to get them to stop but I can't. And as horrible as this is, it's something I wouldn't wish upon my worst enemy."

"Miss De Wet-"

"Please let me finish. When all of this is said and done, I'm sure you'll have a lot of questions, chief among them is why I've decided to help you? If you've decided to call it that. Why I've extended an ear and listened when no one else would, given you a space to vent regardless of what's bothering you and why I've never ever pushed you to try get your Aunt locked up, even though someone outside these four walls might see her as a complete monster and not take into account other circumstances at play. But I'll be honest with you, it would be pretty hard given her position in the police.

Sipho nodded.

Earlier on that day

Palesa was left in the house, alone with nothing to do but clean up after her sister and offspring, watch her favourite soapies and explore. But the things she'd found out about her sister left her in a state of two minds. On the one hand, she was happy for her sister, she'd found someone, someone to make her happy and lead her on the right path towards finding true love if this wasn't the person God had ordained for her. And on the other hand, she wondered why he or she was keeping a secret from her, if Rebecca was indeed dating, it was something one would want to share with someone else unless... her partner was someone else's partner and she was breaking up a happy home.

All these hypothetical questions raced through Palesa's mind as she asked herself but was unable to give answers to. The one person who could answer them was her older sister, she thought, sneaking into her bedroom. It didn't take long for her to find an array of inappropriate outfits, toys and things. She didn't know their names or functions, but she could tell that they had a strange odour. It was a mini adult store she couldn't explain or enquire about. It left her irritated but what could she do, confronting her about it would just cause problems. What happened next could only be Rebecca's doing, there was no other way to explain it. Had she not been hiding her partner, there'd be no need to snoop around the apartment. Meaning she wouldn't have got angry and spring cleaned to cool off, meaning she wouldn't have found her son's letter from school kicking him out. She didn't know what was worse, the secrecy in these four walls due to her sister's deviation on the topic or her son's lies regarding school. All of which meant she needed a drink. Something strong. A sure-fire way to make her forget this betrayal quickly and a task this house bar could not fail at.

11

"Sipho," she sighed, bowing her head. "It's because I've been in a similar position. I was young, the internet was still new, and I'd met this guy. He was a little older than me, only 22 and he convinced me he loved me and I thought he did, but to prove it, I had to send him photos of me, naked. So I did, to prove that I loved him, my 16-year-old self sent naked pictures to a man I'd never met over the internet on a social media network that doesn't exist anymore. But those photos still do. I've tried to get rid of every single picture that's out there, but I don't know for sure if I have. The good news is that he was caught and locked up for child pornography. Others could hide behind my face, so I didn't suffer alone. "And that's how me and my very first boyfriend broke up," she smiled, running her palm across the corner of each eye.

Sipho stared at his teacher, his words from earlier taking on a whole new meaning. "Oh, I'm so sorry I didn't know,"

"Don't be, how could you know? You didn't tell me to send those pictures. Your existence was unknown back then,"

"I'm sorry about what I said earlier. I-"

"Water under the bridge. We can't change the past, we can only change how we let it affect what it does to us in the future," she said, handing him the textbook. "Despite how long it's been, not knowing whether I've rid the internet of my nudes hurts more than having them out there if they do still exist,"

Sipho stood up and gave her a hug, taking her by surprise before she reciprocated it. Carrying papers to sign, Andreas knocked and entered quickly, but confusion and disgust soon followed. Disgust, he could hide well under the veil of professionalism. Personally, he didn't agree with what he saw happen before him. He refused to participate due to his morals and principles... He cleared his throat and untangled student and superior, allowing him to get his irrelevant documents signed.

***

The venue looked like the TV set of a law-based television show. All the props were ready and so were its actors. Andreas couldn't contain himself with excitement, but as the hours crept by until showtime, he had cold feet. He could still pull the plug on this entire operation. Yes, it would have been a waste of many people's time, money and resources and most likely land him in some hot water, but the chances of him getting dismissed were nil too highly unlikely. The actual culprit here was Jolene, not him. Had she agreed to another date, who knows how far along their relationship would be? It sure as hell would be further than where it is now and how God intended it to be, that's for sure. So he promised himself that it was his duty to get rid of her and that little shit she'd come to adore to preserve his and the University's reputation. Words that became clearer when he found a chance to glance across the room and see Sipho seated in isolation on his side of the room. His head hung low, forced to the ground by the brightness of the fluorescent lights above him.

Part of him wanted to walk over and tell him to pick his chin up, whatever was about to happen had nothing to do with him but all of De Wet's doing. Reversely, the boy was in varsity, he should be smart enough to figure it out on his own. By the time their eyes had met, the room had begun to fill up, and he watched as Jolene comforted him no differently to a troubled parent, sending all regret back down faster than acid reflux. With the Dean's arrival, things got underway as he painted a clear picture of how things would proceed. "First, let the record state that Mr Bhengu will not be eligible for the 2020 examinations until the end of this hearing. Should we find him to contravene no rules set out by the

University's code of conduct, his academic year will be based on his term and subsequently yearly average. The plaintiff would present their argument, Mr Coetzee and then the defendants arguing against the claims of sexual assault and harassment presented against them,"

Which made no sense since "Mr Coetzee" wasn't harassed but found a loophole in the University's by-laws to allow him to do this and still have a watertight case to argue the violation of University code of conduct. And so, as the hearing dragged on, Andreas began vomiting his verbal diarrhoea.

"I can attest to the fact that I've caught Ms De Wet and Mr... Bhengu, partaking in teacher-student relations on multiple occasions, a handful of which they were partly or completely undressed, thanks to the wails of ecstasy from Jolene, sorry, Ms De Wet,"

"That's not true!" Sipho yelled.

"Mr Bhengu please," the adjudicator said in a calm voice.

"But he's lying,"

"Yes, he's lying, what more do you want?"

"Quantifiable proof Mr Bhengu, not qualitative,"

Sipho growled as he stared at his fists, looking for a response.

"In the meantime, note down any discrepancies in Mr Coetzee's and Ms De Wet's arguments to rectify these facts when the time comes for you to plead your case, understood?"

"Understood," Sipho mumbled.

"Now, as I was saying before the interruption. I found Mr Bhengu and Ms De Wet in poses that were not fit for any student-lecturer relationship and couldn't be explained even by the most intimate of couples,"

"And why is it you found them and not another passer-by?" Another arbiter asked.

"It was just my like or ordained by God I guess," Andreas replied irritably. Doing something as mundane as buying groceries was a breath of fresh air because it was something different. Something his Aunt and he had never done. Sure, it was surprising when the offer came out of nowhere but it came at a time when two needs intersected that his Aunt could never fulfil if given mere instructions. The first was that he needed some literal fresh air and the second was a specific type of candy he needed to prepare for exams but it was going to be hard, given everything that was going on. So off they went.

...

"Hold the queue, I'll be back, I'm going to grab some of the wine your mother finished before I forget,"

Sipho nodded before wandering with purpose towards the till section.

"Sipho, what a delightful surprise, I wasn't expecting to see you here?" Jolene smiled, opening her arms wide for a hug.

"We're not supposed to be around one another until the end of the trial," Sipho answered, pushing her arms away.

"Well, they can't prove we were here now, can they?" She winked. "Anyway, it was nice seeing you, and smile. I know it might seem like there's nothing to smile about at the moment, but I always find something to do, no matter how small. It's what I've learnt to do since then,"

Sipho nodded before watching what could be his former lecturer walk away with her shopping cart. "Why did you do it?" He asked, calling out to her.

"Do what?"

"Allow him to say all those things about us even though they weren't true?"

"Sipho," she said, returning to him. "I've worked in that university long enough to know who governs and has the last word. The concept of equality is nothing more than a nameplate. If I want to continue with my livelihood as a lecturer and continue to use this grant to finish my research as a psychologist. Then all I can do is bury my head in the sand and wait for all of this to blow over,"

"Psychologist?"

"Yes, Sipho, and a good one at that. Had you taken the time to google me and not just take what I said at face value, you would have found that out pretty quickly. Unfortunately, that lie has been part of the research on human behaviour I've been conducting. It's all a little jarring and hard to believe when you hear it in the middle of a grocery store, especially when you were so on the money about everything I've been doing,"

"But why?"

"I'm human, I'm not perfect, not that you'd believe me now, but besides that little white lie, I've been nothing but honest with you, about everything. I've also told you more than I should have, both about my personal life and this study,"

"I told you to hold the queue. Look at how lo- Is there a problem here... can I help you?" Rebecca asked, holding two bottles of wine.

"No Aunty, everything is okay. In fact, this is my lecturer, Ms De Wet," Sipho said calmly.

After pleasantries were exchanged and the mandatory fake smiles that came with it. Everybody parted their separate ways with their respective groceries. The ride home the topic of De Wet was avoided but Sipho could get a sense that his Aunt wanted to talk about it. Which made sense since she'd avoided the trial for whatever her reasons were, he didn't know, she never gave them to him, not even an excuse for him to use as a stopgap.

12

On the ride home, things returned to normal, as normal as they could be between Sipho and his Aunt, with picking out inanimate objects from shelves and fridges no longer available to distract them.

"How did your hearing go?"

"Going,"

"What?"

"It's ongoing. It hasn't finished," Sipho snapped, rendering the rest of their journey home in silence.

"Sipho, we need to talk about what happened,"

"Nice weather we're having, don't you think?"

"Sipho,"

"I think so, but knowing Bloemfontein, it might rain in the afternoon but you wouldn't be able to tell. The sky is completely blue,"

"Sipho," his Aunt repeated, raising her voice.

"Yes Aunty,"

"I said we need to talk about what happened,"

"There's nothing to talk about,"

"Not this bullshit again. Then where did you get my gun?"

Sipho couldn't answer his Aunt because he didn't have the words. Even if he told her the truth, she wouldn't believe him. The truth was that he'd found it in his room, and the only person who could honestly answer that question was his mother, since she was the one who was left alone in the house all day.

"Sipho, I'm talking to you."

"I want to go see my mother,"

"Not until you tell me where you took my gun from?"

The rest of the trip home was uncomfortable but more so the place he knew as his home. It seemed different, cold and worst of all, were the secrets it hid. It didn't take long for his Aunt to pull out her handcuffs; the silver shined and shimmed as it danced off the light as they approached. Sipho didn't run nor argue but merely gave her his scarred wrists.

"Until you tell me where you got my gun from, you'll sit like this."

***

A stranger could be forgiven for assuming that it was just your typical Aunt and nephew hanging out and streaming a series they both enjoyed on the Tv. But if they had the liberty of peering at what was on the other side of the couch, those handcuffs would unlock an entire set of questions they didn't want the answers to. Rebecca was genuinely surprised at how long Sipho had lasted without giving in to her demands. She knew, however, that eventually, he'd have to eat and use the bathroom. And without fail, the skills of her profession soon paid off.

"I need to go to the bathroom,"

"First, tell me where you took my gun from,"

"Fine. But I can't hold it,"

And with that verbal agreement in place, she let Sipho go. He relieved himself and prepared himself for what was about to ensue. He didn't have time for his Aunt's games and if she kicked him out, then it would be evident that her actions towards his mother weren't a one-time thing propelled by irrational thought and anger. When Sipho returned to the lounge, he sat opposite his Aunt and looked her in the eyes. Not because he'd been instructed to from Master to slave, not as a sign of disrespect directed to his elder but as equals.

"So..."

Before she could even finish her question, Sipho raised a finger, allowing his voice to have inhibited freedom. "I've lived here for three years now and in that time, you've done things you shouldn't have. You've used that gun to scare me into doing those things and used it to make me have sex with you when you knew very well I didn't want to. So of course, I'd know where you'd keep it,"

"So you go digging around in my things as well?"

"No. I've never done that. But as Mom likes to say, for such an organised woman, you're very careless. I don't know what that means. All I know is that you leave things lying around a lot," Sipho shrugged.

Rebecca paused.

Sipho stared at her waiting for her to say something. All he could do was speak when spoken to. What else would he say to her? It's not like there was anything else for her to know.

"So... Where did you take it from before I found you with it?"

"My room,"

"Sipho, don't lie to me. All I want to know is where you found my gun, that's all. I don't know why you want to make this so hard and turn me into someone I'm not,"

"But I'm not lying. I'm telling the truth, that's where I found it," Sipho protested.

"Fine, have it your way. Because you don't want to tell me where you took my gun from, you'll have supper and it's back to handcuffs until you're ready to tell the truth,"

"But-"

"But nothing unless it's the truth," Rebecca instructed before standing up to go dish up.

Halfway through supper, there was a knock on the door, taking both of them by surprise as they exchanged looks with one another. Rebecca attended to the door, not before wedging the handcuffs in-between one of them. She opened the door but regretted it the moment the latch unlocked.

"You're here early,"

"RJ," he chimed. "You know, that's no way to say hello," giving her an unreciprocated hug.

"Hi," Rebecca snapped.

"Would you prefer me to use Jezabel instead?"

"How many times have I told you to stop using my second name?"

"Yeah, I know, but it's fun. Where's everybody?" He asked.

"Isn't that why you're here? To take your wife's shit and get out of my house,"

Sanele walked in, ignoring his sister-in-law's remarks before throwing himself on the couch, not before stealing the meat Sipho was saving to eat last off his plate. "Hey son, how are you? How's school?" He asked through mouthfuls of meat.

"School's fine,"

"You know, driving from KZN was so tiring, it worked up an appetite, I'm so hungry," Sanele said, rubbing his belly. "Rebecca, what's there to eat besides peas, this meat with no salt, you're feeding my son?"

While Sanele ate, all he could do was complain about how Rebecca's healthy living was doing her no good and that her pretending to be a white woman resulted in her cooking food that tastes like cardboard. "I mean, who cooks food with no rice, really? Even Maharaj cooks rice and theirs is yellow. Ching-Chong-Cha's is skinny but white people, nothing. Just like Rebecca," He said, clicking his tongue and placing his plate on the table.

Just like his namesake, Rebecca had had enough of Sanele and showed him the door, and he obliged without putting up much of a fight. His only request was for his son to pack his mother's things since he was now kicked out of the house and for him to join him for some family time before his wife and he made the long trip back down to KZN. He was throwing shit at the fan with that last request and surprised to find it stick. Sipho couldn't be more grateful for the request as it allowed a chance to escape the handcuffs, even if it meant spending time with his father.

•••

It was refreshing to Sipho's taste buds to eat something greasy as father and son drove towards the hotel to reunite as a family. So it came as a surprise to Sipho when his father asked him about his expulsion from school. First, he had to clarify that it wasn't an expulsion, and it was a disciplinary hearing for sexual harassment and assault. It came as more of a shock when his father asked him if he did it. His joking demeanour in his voice absent, but the most shocking thing of all was the fact that it felt as if his father believed him when he gave his answer and told him how he ended up in this situation. For once, after a long time, Sipho felt as though he was with his father, not a man who had fathered him. When they arrived at the hotel, Sipho was happy to see his mother and she was pleased to see him, their last encounter lost in the pages of time. But the addition of Mr Bhengu made it hard to enjoy the moment and caused him to melt away, after all, there was still the unknown ring finger in the room.

13

The disciplinary hearing felt like it went on forever with no foreseeable end. Sipho wished it was a series that would just jump to the most important scenes, like whether he'd be in school next year or not. Unfortunately, this was reality and not a television series, so sitting through the parts of the hearing he didn't want were mandatory. This also gave his father a chance to participate and get clued up on what was happening in his son's life. The person who claimed to be his legal guardian was nowhere to be seen and so he had to go through this ordeal alone until this point. Had it not been for his wife's emotional outburst, who knows what he wouldn't know about his son? He'd be the first to admit that he wasn't the best in raising his son, but this, this was unacceptable. His mother might have neglected her responsibilities, but that didn't mean he had to. Then she'd complain why he wanted to expand his family. All she had to do was be grateful they even informed her of the suggestion. Gumede had married three women in a row, and if she was throwing tantrums with just a trio of legal mistakes, she wouldn't have survived in a much more traditional home compared to his modern interpretation of marriage. But his focus now was on ensuring his son stayed in school and not expulsion.

When Mr Coetzee finished detailing his account of what he'd seen, it meant that Ms De Wet would have to get a perfect score from four white men and a woman added in for good measure to even qualify to be taken seriously. Sipho watched and listened to what the lying psychologist had to say. Nothing stood out of the ordinary, as most of her questions were in line with her occupational history and had nothing to do with her help as a lecturer to a student that needed advice.

"Miss De Wet, can you confirm whether Mr Bhengu assaulted you?" An arbiter asked.

"What is assault?"

"Miss De Wet, can you please answer the question?"

"You know who's responsible for this rape?" she said, facing Andreas.

"Rape?" Andreas blurted out.

Sipho raised his eyes but said nothing, opting to look at his parents in fear and confusion.

"Miss De Wet," the board warned.

"You're white, I'm white... you and I are the same." She continued. "You were meant to be the good in all this evil. My knight in shining armour, save me, protect me, not watch me... watch me get violated," she said, dabbing her eyes.

"Johannes, this is bullshit, this is-" Andreas said, losing control of his voice as Jolene continued explaining why he was the reason she, an innocent white woman who didn't know any better was raped by a savage black boy who found an underhanded way to pass the year.

"Why didn't you report this then?" Andreas asked.

"Yes, why didn't you?" The Dean second.

"Your policies have failed me and allowed me to be taken advantage of on multiple occasions. Had it not been for Andreas and his perversions that allowed him to watch me get violated, repeatedly, it would be happening now as we speak. None of us would be congregated here, where I'm forced to talk about the trauma I've suffered or risk losing my job,"

"This is not true," Andreas said, slamming his hands on his desk as he stood and causing Sipho to flinch.

"But you said it yourself. The words came out of your mouth that you caught us partly or completely naked. You failed to mention the tormented state I was in and how menacing Mr Bhengu was. My mistake is... how simply getting to this point took a lot of willpower because of what it would do to our reputations and the universities,"

"You're twisting my words. I didn't say that. I did, but I didn't mean it like that. What I meant was-"

"No, no," Jolene said, raising a palm to silence him. "You had your chance to speak. Allow me to say this and never hear from me again. This is hard enough to say as it is,"

"Your statements aren't true though. I should know, I know what I saw, and it wasn't rape,"

"Andreas please, calm down,"

"How can I when she's twisting everything I've said to fit her own narrative?"

"I don't seem to understand where the confusion is, why there seems to be some objection to what I'm saying. He was there, he saw it with his own eyes," she said, pointing at Andreas as she faced his pink face. "Are you calling me a liar, or are you one, which one is it?"

"Ladies and gentleman, we will have an hour recess before we commence with the remainder of today's agenda," The Dean said, disappearing behind his colleagues closely followed behind by Andreas.

Sipho spent a good 45 minutes with his family being convinced that nothing would happen to him because he'd done nothing wrong. They'd never stepped foot in Jolene De Wet's office, but what they knew with certainty was that they didn't raise a rapist. Andreas spent most of that hour smoking and being reminded by Johannes to tone it down or he'd put himself in a position that even he couldn't rescue him from. All he had to do was to remain calm and allow Johannes to prove Jolene's story otherwise. The hearing soon resumed after a breath of fresh air, found new vigour in its execution. Not long after it started, Rebecca entered with a lady in a pinstriped suit behind her, causing irritated faces all around at another disruption.

"May I ask what's the meaning of this is?" A board member demanded.

They ignored him as the ladies found Sipho, who then pointed to his parents before they murmured sweet nothings to each other as Rebecca sat down. The lady in the pinstriped suit was the only objective entity in the entire room as she informed everyone of what was going on, providing some much-needed clarification including to Sipho who was blindsided by his Aunt's actions.

"My name is Noluntu Ntuli, and I am Sipho Bhengu's legal representative. Everything my client has said prior to legal representation is invalid, as stipulated in your own code of conduct. It entitles my client to legal representation and if he cannot get it, the institution shall provide him with a legal representative shall he request it. This means, given all the paperwork I've had to sift through until this point, you've contravened your own bylaws by not making him aware of his rights,"

This woman was on fire. There was no way they'd be taking chances with him now, Sipho thought to himself. He turned around to glance at the person who made all of this happen and what made her emerge from her sudden absence. But his positivity was short-lived. His Aunt and mother sat yards apart from one another, making it visible to anybody with two brain cells to rub together that something was wrong. And it's not like his father could try to reconcile any differences they had having burnt bridges with both of them. As much as Sipho appreciated that his family was finally here to support him, he thought he was better off alone because his family issues being aired out in public were the last thing he needed, if ever. And with that, the trial continued, with the questions that were meant to reveal Jolene as a fraud and a liar being used to chip away at Andreas's accusations.

...

"So are you saying they did not rape me?" Jolene asked.

"Not this shit again. I told you, that's not what happened between the two of you. You took it as far as second base, max,"

"Shut up," the Dean hissed.

"Do you agree to being sexually assaulted?" Another of the adjudicators asked.

"Your question is very misleading," she said, before focusing her attention on everybody in the room in front of her. "Do you think I'd play around with something as serious as gender-based violence? How moronic do you think I am, or better yet, are you to have such a lack of empathy for other human beings?"

The room fell quiet, allowing for the crack in Jolene's voice to be amplified even more as she began to cry. "Do any of you here know what it feels like to be handcuffed? To take part in something without your consent, with nothing but a gun to remind you of what happens when you say no. To be forced to wear sexual garments, come to work looking like a teacher, but in your office, strip down to nothing more than chains and whips to entertain nothing more than the sexual fantasies of a sick, twisted mind. To be chained to a desk and made to feel like nothing more than an object. I have, and it's all because of him," she said in-between sobs, pointing at Sipho.

As Jolene's red nail polished finger pointed at Sipho like a laser, he looked back at his family without hesitation, guiding it on where to go. His eyes danced with his Aunts who felt betrayed that he'd shared what they did behind closed doors with the world, who herself could feel the glare emanate from her sister as she put two and two together. Watching her son stare at her sister and the effect his lecture's words had on them. The clothes, the toys, the mystery boyfriend? the answer to that question disturbed her mentally and took all of her senses with it. What Rebecca couldn't see was the regret her actions had caused, questions of how she claimed to love Sipho like her own child but do such a thing. The same child Palesa had left her with in order for it to have a better education. But as Sipho's eyes finished wandering from parent to parent and focused back onto the one person he'd trusted, who betrayed him not once but twice and blinded him with the darkest parts of him while doing it. Jolene De Wet.

"Ms De Wet, please answer the question, were you or were you not raped by the defendant?"

"I can't remember,"

"Sorry, come again?"

To be continued.

Don't miss out!

Visit the website below and you can sign up to receive emails whenever Londa Cele publishes a new book. There's no charge and no obligation.

https://books2read.com/r/B-A-XGKG-CTBHC

BOOKS2READ

Connecting independent readers to independent writers.

Also by Londa Cele

The Gifted
Someone New
Angels of Death

Unsupervised
Questionable Decisions

Standalone
Nomalungelo
Wedding Vows
Thando's Strength
Extra Lessons

Watch for more at www.londacelenovelz.wordpress.com.

About the Author

Londa Cele is the founder of LondaCeleNovels and the author of Nomalungelo & Wedding Vows. Graduate of SA Writer's College and Toastmaster's recipient, but a shy one at that. Londa currently resides in South Africa and is fluent in 5 languages.

Follow him on Twitter @Londa_Cele

Read more at www.londacelenovelz.wordpress.com.